THE BULLS VS. THE TEACHERS!

"Well, guys," Mr. Earl asked, "what do you think of our faculty team?"

"Mr. Earl, no offense," Dave finally replied. "But you call the group of klutzes you had out on the floor a *team?*"

Mr. Earl smiled patiently. "I was thinking about what Brian was saying to me the other day—about the Bulls being able to crush the teachers in a game. So I invited a few of my faculty friends to play, including Dr. Byrum here."

"I suppose we *could* use a little more practice," Dr. Byrum added.

"But if you really think you can take us," Mr. Earl said, "we're up for it."

Brian thought about how easy it would be to steal the ball from Ms. Darling. How much fun it would be to go head-to-head with Mr. Earl. Of course, Mr. O'Shea would also be playing.

"You want us, you got us!" Brian heard Will bellow.

HANG
TIME

by
Hank Herman

BANTAM BOOKS
NEW YORK · TORONTO · LONDON · SYDNEY · AUCKLAND

RL 2.6, 007-010

HANG TIME

A Bantam Book / February 1997

Produced by Daniel Weiss Associates, Inc.
33 West 17th Street
New York, NY 10011.

Cover art by Jeff Mangiat.

ISBN: 0-553-48431-1
Published simultaneously in the United States and Canada

Bantam Books are published by Bantam Books, a division of Bantam
Doubleday Dell Publishing Group, Inc. Its trademark, consisting of the
words "Bantam Books" and the portrayal of a rooster, is Registered in U.S.
Patent and Trademark Office and in other countries. Marca Registrada.
Bantam Books, 1540 Broadway, New York, New York 10036.

PRINTED IN THE UNITED STATES OF AMERICA

OPM   0 9 8 7 6 5 4 3 2 1

To Robby, future all-American

CHAPTER 1

Brian Simmons stood at mid-court, the ball cradled in the crook of his right arm, his dark eyes on the hoop. He took a deep breath, then started into his dribble. After crossing the foul line he leaped toward the basket, faked a dish to his left, and then scooped the ball underhanded up over the front rim.

MJ, a gawky African American kid who wore white wraparound goggles, hit the button on his fancy digital stopwatch. "Point-eight seconds," he said.

"Point-eight!" David Danzig crowed. "I can beat that—easy!"

"Point-eight seconds—no way!" Brian screeched in return, as he brushed the sweat from his fade haircut with the back of his hand. "I was in the air for a full second, *at least*. You ought to go get yourself a new watch!"

Brian, MJ, and Dave were all members of the Branford Bulls, a team of basketball-crazy fifth-graders. They were also in the same gym class at Benjamin Franklin Middle School. For the last few weeks they'd been competing in a "hang time" contest before the class actually got under way. Mr. Earl, their gym teacher, always let the kids goof around for a few minutes before he'd blow the whistle, calling them together for jumping jacks. Brian could tell that

Mr. Earl really knew what kids liked. That was just one of the many reasons he was Brian's favorite teacher in the school.

Dave's turn was next. He shook his long blond hair out of his eyes, dribbled a few times between his legs, and then soared to the hoop. In the air, he pumped twice but didn't have enough momentum left to send the ball up to the basket.

"One-point-two seconds hang time—but no bucket. Disqualified!" MJ announced.

"Hey, I thought we were just judging hang time and style points," Dave squawked. "Who cares if the ball goes in?"

"That's Droopy all over," Brian said with a smirk, using Dave's nickname. "Doesn't matter how he plays—as long as his move looks good, his hair looks good, and his shorts are hanging down below his knees."

"Stand back, you two, this thing's not over yet," MJ warned.

Brian shook his head and smiled to himself. MJ, whose real name—unbelievably—was Michael Jordan, was by far the least athletic of all the Branford Bulls. Fortunately, he *knew* the game inside out, and that made up, at least a little, for his lack of co-ordination. One way or another, he managed to contribute to the Bulls' victories. *Somehow, though, I don't see him winning a hang time contest,* Brian thought.

Sure enough, just before taking off for the basket, MJ got his feet all tangled up. The ball squirted out of his hands as he crashed headlong into the blue tumbling mat that hung behind the basket for just such occasions.

"Minus two seconds in the air," Brian laughed, clicking an imaginary watch, "but nine-point-nine points for style. Hey, dude, you all right?"

"He's fine, he's fine," Mr. Earl answered for MJ, extending a hand to help pull MJ up off the floor. "He just dented the wall a little bit." The teacher had been heading to the end of the gym where the Bulls were playing when MJ took his spill.

"Who would notice?" Dave wisecracked. "This gym is in such bad shape, what's another dent in the wall?"

Mr. Earl ignored Dave's complaint. Everyone knew the BFMS gym could stand some serious fixing up.

"Hey, aren't you guys using the wrong kind of ball?" Mr. Earl asked. "We're playing flag football today."

Brian, Dave, and MJ all winced, as if to ask, *Why football?*

"Oh, I forgot," Mr. Earl said with a smile. "You guys are the *Bulls*. And basketball's always in season for the Bulls."

"You got that right!" Dave called out enthusiastically. "Hey, Mr. Earl, watch this." Dave picked the ball up from the floor, took a few steps back toward mid-court, then dribbled to the basket and performed the same double-clutch move as before. But this time he was able to make the basket.

"Ever see hang time like that, Mr. Earl?" Dave boasted.

"Not since Dr. J. But here, check this out." Mr. Earl grabbed the ball from Dave and backed away from the hoop, giving himself room.

As the gym teacher got ready for his attempt, Brian studied him. Mr. Earl had dark black skin, close-cropped hair, and was about five-foot-eight. He had bulging biceps, a big barrel of a chest, and a narrow waist. Brian had heard from other teachers that Mr. Earl was sixty years old, but he couldn't believe it: The man was in such great shape! Brian also guessed, from the gym teacher's build and from the silky way he carried himself, that he'd probably been quite an athlete in his day.

Mr. Earl drove hard to the hoop. He threw a ball fake the way the boys had done and made a nice finger roll over the front rim. But for all his grace, the gym teacher's feet never really left the floor.

Brian, Dave, and MJ snickered. "This is a *hang time* contest, Mr. Earl," Dave said. "You barely even got off the ground."

"Yeah, I hate to say it, Mr. Earl," Brian chimed in, "but if you gym teachers are the best ballplayers in the school, I'd hate to watch the rest of the teachers play! The Branford Bulls could *crush* you guys in a game."

Mr. Earl's only reaction to the dis was a very slight raising of his eyebrows. Finally the teacher said, "Is that so?"

As the boys were heading out of the gym after the flag football game, Brian spotted Mr. O'Shea casually leaning against the doorway, looking as if he were posing for an Old Spice ad. His hair was slicked back and his face was tanned. Brian got the distinct impression that the young teacher thought of himself as a pretty handsome guy.

Brian knew that besides teaching gym at BFMS, Mr. O'Shea also coached a very successful ninth-grade prep school basketball team in Danville, a neighboring town. Brian found himself resenting Mr. O'Shea, with his too-cool attitude.

Who does he think he is, the next Pat Riley? If he only knew how much the kids at this school hate him, Brian thought. As popular as Mr. Earl was, that's how *un*popular Mr. O'Shea was. The other Bulls who went to BFMS—Will, Derek, Chunky, and Mark—all had Mr. O'Shea as their gym teacher. They couldn't stand him. Everyone thought of him as a stuck-up know-it-all.

For some reason, the only person in the school Mr. O'Shea seemed to respect—or fear—was Mr. Earl.

Brian brushed by the gym teacher as he exited the gym. "Mr. Simmons, can I see you for a second?" Mr. O'Shea asked sternly.

Brian's heart sunk. What was it *this* time? He'd already had a run-in with Mr. O'Shea the first week of school, when Mr. O'Shea had sent him to the principal's office for wearing his red Bulls' jersey to gym class instead of the required white T-shirt. And the teacher had seemed to have it in for him ever since.

Mr. O'Shea put his face right up to Brian's—so close that Brian could see the tiny stubble of beard growing back on the teacher's clean-shaven chin.

"You think you're pretty hot stuff, don't you, Mr. Simmons?" Mr. O'Shea asked. It was pretty obvious that the gym teacher was angry at him for *something,* but Brian honestly had no idea what it might be.

"I happened to catch your conversation with Mr. Earl at the beginning of class," Mr. O'Shea explained. "You remember, when you were making fun of him and the rest of us teachers here at BFMS?"

"I wasn't making fun—," Brian began, his face turning red, but Mr. O'Shea cut him off.

"I'll have you know that some of the faculty here can play quite well, thank you," Mr. O'Shea continued. "Maybe Mr. Earl lets you get away with that kind of mouthing off, but *I* don't."

"I didn't mean—"

"In the future," Mr. O'Shea cut in again, "I'd like to see *all* the teachers here at BFMS treated with a little more respect than you showed Mr. Earl before."

Brian tried to explain one more time that what he'd said to the older gym teacher was just good-natured kidding, but Mr. O'Shea had already stalked off down the hallway.

CHAPTER 2

"What do you think your brother will have us working on at practice today?" Brian asked Will. The two boys, along with Dave and MJ, were stuffing their books in their backpacks and pulling their jackets out of their lockers.

Will smirked. "Probably something boring, like the zone press," he answered. Will Hopwood, one of the original members of the Bulls along with Brian and Dave, was the tallest kid on the team, and one of the most talented. His older brother, Jim, a star guard for the Branford High varsity team, was one of the Bulls' two teenage coaches.

"What's boring about practicing the zone press?" MJ asked. Brian smiled. MJ found *everything* about basketball interesting. The coaches, Jim and Nate Bowman, Jr., often referred to MJ as a "student of the game." *Good thing he's a student,* Brian thought, *because he sure isn't much of a player!*

"Hey, whatever," Dave added. "At least we'll be playing *basketball.* I've had enough of *this* place for one day." By *this place,* of course, he meant *school.* Brian couldn't agree with him more.

MJ began grabbing everything out of his locker in alarm. He had an anxious look on his face. "Hey, I can't find my watch," he said. "I'll bet I left it in the gym. Let's head through there on the way to the bus."

The four Bulls hustled through the hall toward the gym, but when they got to the entrance, they stopped short.

Will's jaw dropped, and his eyes

opened wide. "What the . . . ," he said in disbelief.

The Bulls had expected to find an empty gym, but it wasn't empty at all. It was full of teachers.

Teachers trying to play *basketball*.

"No way!" Dave sputtered, covering his mouth to contain his laughter. "Is that *Ms. Darling?*"

It *was* Ms. Darling, their short, spunky English teacher. The boys were used to seeing the pretty teacher in a dress. Now she was wearing cutoff blue jeans and an extra-large T-shirt. She slapped at the ball with two hands at once. Brian remembered seeing his three-year-old cousin Darryl bouncing the ball the same way.

"Hey, Droopy," Brian called out to Dave, "Ms. Darling learn that dribbling technique from you?" Brian loved to tease Dave. Though Dave and another teammate, Jo Meyerson, were easily the best ball handlers on the Bulls— and among the best in the league— Dave was still sensitive to needling.

"Yeah," Dave shot back, "and it looks like Mr. Dupont over there modeled *his* game after *you!*"

The Bulls followed Dave's glance and broke into hysterics. If Ms. Darling looked funny in her oversized T-shirt, Mr. Dupont, the tall, skinny social studies teacher, looked *ridiculous*. He wore his shiny blue satin shorts very short and very tight, the way the NBA players wore them back in the old days. His white socks were pulled way up to his knees, making his legs look like stilts. And he shot an old-fashioned, two-handed set shot, starting the motion from down in front of his belly button.

"The amazing part," Will choked, trying to keep his voice down so the teachers couldn't hear, "is that Mr. Dupont really thinks he looks cool. You should hear him talk about his game in class. You'd think he used to be Larry Bird or something. He once told me he won a statewide free-throw shooting contest back in Delaware."

"They must have some pretty awful free-throw shooters in Delaware!" MJ hooted.

"Wait—now here's a man who can hit his foul shots," Dave remarked. A short, white-bearded man wearing black gym shorts and a plain gray T-shirt was at the line, hitting shot after shot. "Man, Dr. Byrum's *automatic*," Dave said admiringly. "He's just like me!"

Dr. Byrum was the popular principal of Benjamin Franklin Middle School. He was so easygoing and had such a good sense of humor that the students didn't consider being sent to the principal's office to be that big of a punishment.

"Yeah, but I think I've found a weakness in his game," MJ observed.

When they saw what MJ meant, the Bulls burst out laughing once again.

Dr. Byrum had been fine when the other teachers were passing him the ball at the foul line. But it was another story when he had to bend over and retrieve a ball himself. His belly was so big that he had trouble reaching the floor. Dr. Byrum made Nate's dad, Mr. Bowman, the roly-poly owner of Bowman's Market, look slim.

Next the boys spotted Mr. Charles—who was about as unlikely-looking a basketball player as any of them had ever seen. The short, squat math teacher wore thick, black-framed glasses. He also had on plaid Bermuda shorts and thin black socks. His white legs looked as though they'd never been out in the sun.

Will dropped his backpack where he stood and bounded onto the court. He couldn't resist the urge to show off. "Yo, let's show these teachers what's up!" he called.

He strode over to the near foul line, where Ms. Darling was still trying to dribble. Will, at five-foot-four, was

three inches taller than
the tiny English teacher.
With hardly any effort,
he stole the ball from
her. A moment later, he
gracefully swished a
turnaround jumper, his
trademark shot.

"Will Hopwood!" Ms.
Darling scolded, "That
was my ball!"

"*Was* is right," Dave laughed. "It
isn't anymore!" Dave, Brian, and MJ
had followed Will onto the court.
Dave had grabbed a rebound and now
dribbled as he spoke. He sent the ball
behind his back, between his legs, always in perfect control—as if the ball
were on a string.

"The idea is to keep the ball low,"
Dave instructed Ms. Darling, "and to
protect it with your body. That way
you won't get it stolen." Dave allowed
his dribble to go high, tempting the
English teacher to go for the steal.

"Don't be so sure of yourself,

hotshot," Ms. Darling warned as she grabbed for the ball.

But just as the English teacher lunged, Dave went into his low speed-dribble, so the only thing she captured was air.

Brian, from off in the corner of the court, smiled at her frustration. "Ms. Darling," he said, "you're the best at explaining the themes of *The Witch of Blackbird Pond*, but somehow you don't look real at home on the basketball court."

As he spoke, a stray ball rolled out to him. Brian picked it up and, almost effortlessly, canned an eighteen-footer from the corner. "See?" he said to Ms. Darling. "Simple."

"Easy for you to say," Ms. Darling answered, shaking her head and smiling.

Just then Brian saw Will start rolling to the hoop. Dave, who seemed to be gazing in the opposite direction, shot him a behind-the-back, no-look pass. Will caught it in full stride, sailed under the basket, and made a reverse layup.

By now, Ms. Darling, Mr. Dupont, Dr. Byrum, and Mr. Charles had stopped playing and were watching the Bulls put on their display. Brian could tell the teachers were impressed. The only two who didn't seem to be interested were Mr. Earl and Mr. O'Shea. They continued to practice at the other basket. Although he wasn't thrilled about seeing Mr.

O'Shea again, Brian strolled down to that end of the court.

Mr. Earl played exactly the way Brian would have expected. He made a fair percentage of his shots, which he took mostly from close range. He dribbled well. Nothing fancy. No nonsense.

Mr. O'Shea was another story. Though Brian hated to admit it, the younger gym teacher really could *play*. During one stretch of less than a minute, he soared to tap in a missed shot by Mr. Earl, snared a rebound with one hand, and made a gorgeous spin move in the lane. The last one really impressed Brian.

Trying to get back on Mr. O'Shea's good side, he said, "Man, you took that one right out of the Michael Jordan highlight film!"

But Mr. O'Shea took the remark the wrong way. He shot Brian a nasty look. "Watch the sarcasm, Mr. Simmons," he snapped. "I've already given you *one* warning about that attitude of yours."

Brian felt his face get hot. He couldn't believe it! *Why is it that every time I open my mouth around Mr. O'Shea,* he thought, *I put my foot in it?*

CHAPTER 3

"Hey, guys," Will said, rushing to the sideline for his backpack. "We better get our stuff before the bus leaves without us. You know what a prince my brother can be when we're late for practice."

"I'm ready," MJ added. "I found my watch in my gym locker, right where I left it."

Brian wiped his face with his T-shirt. Dave tossed his head, and Brian saw the sweat fly from Dave's long blond hair. They headed for the en-trance to the gym where they had dumped their backpacks and jackets.

"Yeah," Dave agreed, "we ought to hit the road. I think we've given these teachers enough schooling for one day."

As the Bulls gathered up their belongings, Mr. Earl and Dr. Byrum strolled over to them. Mr. Earl said with a twinkle in his eye, "Well guys, what do you think of our faculty team?"

Dave threw himself to the ground, pretending to pass out.

"Mr. Earl, Dr. Byrum, no offense," he finally said, as if he had regained consciousness. "But you call that group of klutzes you just had out on the floor a *team?*"

While Dr. Byrum rolled his eyes, Mr. Earl smiled patiently. He answered in a matter-of-fact tone, "I was thinking about what Brian was saying to me earlier today—about the Bulls being able to crush the teachers in a game. So I invited a few of my faculty friends together, including Dr. Byrum here."

"I suppose we *could* use a little

more practice," Dr. Byrum added.

"But if you really think you can take us," Mr. Earl said, "we're up for it." Mr. Earl was looking directly at Brian as he issued the challenge.

Brian thought about how easy it would be to steal the ball from Ms. Darling. How satisfying it would be to stuff Mr. Dupont or Dr. Byrum. How much fun it would be to go head-to-head with Mr. Earl. Of course, Mr. O'Shea would also be playing. . . .

"You want us, you got us!" Brian heard Will bellow before he had the chance to respond to Mr. Earl and Dr. Byrum himself.

"But it won't be pretty," Dave boasted. "I mean, you *did* see us play with your own eyes. Don't say we didn't warn you."

"Then it's a done deal," Mr. Earl said evenly. "Friday night, right here at the BFMS gym."

"And to sweeten the pot a little," Dr. Byrum put in, "we'll charge two dollars admission, and use the money to fix up the old gym Mr. Earl tells me you guys are always whining about."

Brian's face brightened at the idea of using the game as a fund-raiser. Then another thought hit him.

"One more thing," he said excitedly. "How 'bout if the Bulls win, we all get A's in gym this quarter?"

Dr. Byrum just rolled his eyes again.

Mr. Earl folded his huge arms in front of his chest and smiled. "You know I can't do that, Simmons," he said. "But my old friend Mr. Bowman tells me you Bulls always go over to his shop to cool off after a game. Why don't we play for sodas—losers pay."

"You're on!" Brian shouted, slapping the gym teacher a high five.

Brian, Dave, Will, and MJ turned through the stone pillars into Jefferson Park and hurried down the narrow, paved walk to the blacktop court where they always practiced. From a distance, Brian could see the other four Bulls—Jo Meyerson, Derek Roberts, Mark Fisher, and Chunky Schwartz—already shooting around. Jim and Nate, the coaches, were there too, standing on the sideline.

As Brian and his group reached the blacktop, Nate had his arms folded in front of him and a glad-you-could-finally-make-it expression on his face. Jim looked at his wristwatch meaningfully.

Mark, a short kid with curly, dirty blond hair and wraparound goggles, said, "Where were you guys? Looking for Dave's jump shot?" He had a wise-guy smirk on his face.

"At least I *have* a jumper," Dave countered. "Not that ugly, one-handed prayer of yours that you call a shot."

Mark, who was holding the ball just above the top of the key, obligingly hoisted one up. It was an awkward, shot put–like heave, just as Dave had described. Amazingly, though, it fell cleanly through the hoop.

Will totally ignored Mark's shooting dis-  play. "Sorry we're late," he said, "but we've got some awe- some news. We just got challenged to a game Friday night!"

"Friday night?" Jim objected. "But we've got a game early Saturday morning against Essex—"

"Calm down, Big Bro," Will inter- rupted. "It's only against the Ben Franklin teachers. We just watched them play, and I guarantee—we could beat them blindfolded, with one hand tied behind our backs!"

Nate's face lit up with a big smile. Brian could see that he relished the idea. But Jim still looked concerned. Brian tried to reassure him.

"You really don't need to worry," Brian said. "We won't even break a sweat, I promise. I mean, the teachers are *awful!*"

Chunky, the wide-bodied backup center and one of the few Bulls who suffered from underconfidence, said timidly, "Maybe *you* think they stink, but they're still grown-ups. They're still a lot bigger than we are."

"Chunky, not many of them are bigger than *you*," Dave responded. You *tower* over Ms. Darling, and even though Mr. Dupont is tall, he, well—"

"He couldn't drive to the hoop if you gave him directions," Will said, finishing Dave's sentence for him.

Jo stood on the edge of the black-top, casually spin-ning a basketball on her right index finger. She wore her green baseball cap backward, as 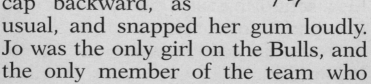 usual, and snapped her gum loudly. Jo was the only girl on the Bulls, and the only member of the team who didn't live in Branford. But even though she came from Sampton, Jo knew most of the Branford teachers, just from hanging around with the Bulls.

"I'll bet Mr. Earl is pretty good," Jo offered. "I've heard that old guy's got an incredible build."

Nate chuckled knowingly. "Mr. Earl pumps some serious iron," the seventeen-year-old said, "but hoops isn't really his thing. Back when I was at BFMS, I used to play him one-on-one every so often." He shook his head mournfully. "Destroyed the dude every time."

Coming from most other teenagers, Brian would have dismissed the boasting as just big talk. But Nate Bowman, Jr., with his gold stud earring and his size-seventeen sneakers, was widely recognized as the best high-school basketball player in Danville County. He not only talked the talk, he walked the walk. Brian believed him.

"Besides," Nate continued, palming a basketball in his huge right hand, "Mr. Earl's got to be sixty years old, at least. You guys have the young legs."

As he mentioned "young legs," Nate roared to the near hoop and threw down a monstrous jam. No matter how many times Brian saw him do that, he was still impressed.

Throughout the whole discussion, Derek Roberts, a reed-thin African American who wore red-white-and-blue wristbands and moved with the grace of a young Scottie Pippen, kept shooting jumpers from ten to fifteen feet. He made an astounding percentage of them.

Brian thought he heard Derek mumble something. He asked him to repeat it.

"Mr. O'Shea," the quietest Bull said, without expression.

"What about Mr. O'Shea?" Brian asked, his interest piqued.

"Dude can play," Derek said simply. Then he drained another twelve-footer.

Brian swallowed hard. Derek always knew what was up. *So Derek is impressed by Mr. O'Shea too,* Brian thought. *That's great! And Mr. O'Shea already thinks I have an attitude. If we play the teachers Friday night, guess who Mr. O'Shea's going to want to guard. . . .*

Though the thought troubled Brian, he decided he wasn't going to let his problems with Mr. O'Shea spoil his anticipation of the upcoming challenge game. He grabbed a loose ball from the grass along the edge of the blacktop and dribbled into the left corner—his sweet spot. Then he released a soft fadeaway jumper.

The perfect shot pumped him up again.

"No way a team featuring the ball handling of Ms. Darling and the hang time of Mr. Earl is going to beat the Bulls!" Brian promised.

CHAPTER 4

Dave had MJ pinned in the corner of the court. If MJ tried to move at all, he'd be forced to step out of bounds over either the sideline or the endline. And with Dave's arms waving wildly in front of his face, Brian knew that MJ's chances of hitting Will with a pass were pretty slim.

The Bulls had finally had enough of their hang time contest and were now using the few minutes of goofing around Mr. Earl allowed them at the beginning of gym class to play two-on-two—MJ and Will versus Dave and Brian. Of course, it wasn't easy to keep the game going with about fifty other kids playing tag, kickball, and knockout all on the same gym floor.

Just before MJ lost his balance and began toppling out of bounds, he called out, "Hey, Mr. Earl!"

As Dave turned around to see the gym teacher, MJ quickly fired a pass to Will under the hoop. Using his height advantage, Will scored easily on a short jumper over Brian.

MJ sat on the hard wood floor, where he'd fallen after making the successful pass. He had a huge, satisfied grin on his face.

"That was pretty cheesy!" Dave howled. "I had you totally trapped!"

"Hey," MJ laughed, "you know I'm not quite as talented as some of you superstars." He tapped himself on the side of the head. "I have to use what's up here."

MJ reached out his hand—an invitation for Dave to help him off the floor, but Dave waved him off. "Get up yourself!" Dave muttered.

Will came over and tugged his teammate upright, so the game could resume. Since they were playing loser's out, Brian checked the ball with Will, then inbounded to Dave.

Brian could see that Dave was still aggravated over MJ's sneaky play and now was trying to get back at him by keeping the ball away with a fancy dribbling exhibition. Dave was Brian's best friend, but sometimes the blond-haired boy's attitude annoyed him. *Why does he always have to be such a hot dog?* Brian wondered. *That kind of showing off always gets him into trouble.*

Sure enough, Dave got careless and allowed his dribble to get too high.

MJ flashed his right hand out, knocked the ball loose, and grasped it to his body with both hands. Surprised that he'd been able to strip the ball from Dave, he rushed up an awkward heave, without even getting a look at the basket.

The shot bricked off the backboard, and Dave, recovering quickly from his embarrassment, positioned himself perfectly to grab the rebound. Then he immediately kicked the ball out to Brian.

Brian looked down at his feet to make sure he was positioned outside the three-point circle, then let loose a high-arching rainbow shot.

"Simmons for three!" Brian sang, jabbing the

middle three fingers of his right hand in the air.

"Sorry, Simmons, make that *two*. Your foot was on the line."

Recognizing the voice of Mr. Earl, Brian whirled around to face him.

"Are you kidding?" Brian screeched. "I was five feet behind the—"

"Gotcha!" Mr. Earl crowed, pointing at Brian and grinning ear to ear. "Man, you *do* take your hoops seriously!"

A smile spread across Brian's face. He couldn't believe he'd fallen for that one. Mr. Earl was always pulling little tricks—he was just like one of the kids. It was another thing Brian liked about him so much.

"Listen," Mr. Earl continued, "I'm glad I have all you Bulls together before I get the class going on calisthenics. I've got a small bit of bad news for you—"

"I knew it!" Brian interrupted, punching his left palm with his right fist. "The game is off, right? Man, everybody in school was totally psyched about it—"

"No, no, calm down, Simmons," Mr. Earl interrupted. "It's just that I've been called in as a speaker at a phys ed teachers' convention in Chicago, so, unfortunately, I'll have to miss the game. But—"

"Then the game *is* off, like Brian said!" Dave cut in. "What's the point of playing if you're not there?"

"Guys, would you please let me finish? What I'm trying to say is that you don't have to worry; the game will go on fine without me. Mr. O'Shea will step in and run the faculty team. I've already spoken with him and it's all arranged—"

"*Mr. O'Shea?*" Brian asked, stricken. He felt his stomach muscles tighten up. *Mr. O'Shea hates my guts*, Brian thought. *How could Mr. Earl not know that?* Besides, this game wasn't just about playing the faculty. It was about playing against Mr. Earl and showing off their stuff to him in front of the whole school. Now it wouldn't be the same at all. . . .

"How 'bout we just push the whole thing back to next Friday?" Brian offered desperately.

"No," Mr. Earl answered, shaking his head. "I've already reserved the gym for this Friday. It's all set up, and everybody's looking forward to it. I've had students asking me about the game all day. And don't forget—we'll be raising money to fix up the gym. You go ahead and have a great time."

Oh, yeah, it'll be great—just great, Brian thought bitterly.

How could he explain to Mr. Earl what he was feeling? It wasn't only that Mr. O'Shea obviously had it in for him—though that was bad enough. He just didn't seem to like *any* of the kids. All Mr. O'Shea cared about was himself. Brian hung his head and walked slowly to his place in line for calisthenics.

As Brian started doing his jumping jacks, a guy on his right called, "Hey, Simmons! Can't wait to see your team trash the teachers!" But even his classmate's excitement couldn't cheer him up.

Though he didn't know exactly how it was going to happen, Brian felt certain of one thing: With Mr. O'Shea coaching the faculty team, the game the Bulls had been looking forward to so much was going to be a *disaster*.

CHAPTER 5

"Can we stay and watch the game?" Todd called out from the back row of seats, as Mr. Simmons pulled the minivan into the parking lot at Benjamin Franklin Middle School.

"Yeah, we want to see Bri-Bri stuff those teachers!" Allie chimed in, her voice almost identical to her twin's.

Todd and Allie were Brian's little brother and sister. The eight-year-olds hung out with the Bulls whenever they could. For third-graders, they were pretty cool kids, and the Bulls didn't mind having them around.

Since they spent so much time with Brian and his friends, Todd and Allie probably knew more about basketball than any other eight-year-olds in the town of Branford.

"Of course, we're all going to stay," Mrs. Simmons answered. She slid open the door of the minivan to let the little ones out. "We wouldn't miss this game for anything!"

Brian had noticed that *everyone* was excited about the fund-raiser game. Even he, despite his misgivings, had managed to get psyched. Mr. Earl couldn't be there, and that was that. At least Ms. Darling, Mr. Dupont, and Dr. Byrum—three members of the faculty he really liked—would be playing. He'd decided to make the best of it.

Brian walked through the double doors into the gym and could hardly believe his eyes. The bleachers were packed! Though he'd heard a lot of talk about the game that day in school, he had no idea it would be such a big attraction. At the regular

Bulls' games, there usually were a handful of people in the bleachers: parents, brothers and sisters, a few friends, maybe even some kids from other teams in the league. But a full house—that was something that only happened for championship games!

The first spectator Brian recognized was Mr. Bowman, the most loyal Bulls' fan of all, sitting beside Mr. and Mrs. Hopwood and a few other parents. He also spotted a group of girls from his homeroom. They were sitting at mid-court, about halfway up the bleachers. Kristen Albert, who called him on the phone all the time, was one of them. Brian had to admit she was kind of cute, but he found it embarrassing how forward she was: She referred to him as her *boyfriend*—even when his teammates were around!

Kristen and her friends were holding up a big poster that said Go Bulls! Well, that was no surprise. Brian couldn't imagine that any of the kids would be rooting for the teachers!

He saw a group of his teammates clustered on the sideline and sauntered over to them, feeling pretty important in his red-and-black Bulls jersey. They seemed much more subdued than usual. Even Dave, who normally would be mouthing off before a game, had a concerned look on his face.

"What's up, guys?" Brian asked, starting to feel worried.

Dave didn't answer. He just nodded in the direction of the hoop at the other end of the gym, where the teachers were warming up.

Brian saw a bunch of adults he didn't recognize shooting around. He looked hard, trying to find some familiar faces. Finally he spotted Ms. Darling, Mr. Dupont, and Dr. Byrum, all sitting glumly on the bench. Mr. Charles was standing near the basket, but nobody was passing him the ball.

Brian felt a queasy sensation in his stomach. Seeing three teachers he knew glued to the bench and staring down at their sneakers was not a good sign. *Why can't Mr. Earl be here tonight?* Brian found himself wondering, even though he'd promised himself not to worry about that.

Chunky pointed at a short, athletic-looking man with tight, curly black hair who was wearing the white BFMS T-shirt the teachers had apparently chosen as their uniform, and red gym shorts.

"Man, would you look at him dribble!" Chunky said in awe. "He makes Dave and Jo look like scrubs. No offense." Chunky looked over at the Bulls' two best ball handlers, to make sure they didn't take what he'd said as an insult.

"Forget the dribbling—look at him sky!" Jo added. She was too impressed by the player's leaping ability to be offended. "That guy can almost dunk, and he's probably not more than five-eight!"

Mark was looking off in another direction. "What about that tall dude in the corner, shooting J's?" he asked. "I haven't seen him miss!"

Brian shifted his gaze to where Mark was looking and saw an African American man, about six-foot-four, stroking jumper after jumper from about eighteen feet out.

After another minute or two of mute staring, Will finally asked, "Who *are* these guys?"

It was exactly what Brian was wondering.

"Yeah, since when does the BFMS faculty have so many jocks?" Mark wanted to know.

"How can we match up against a team like that?" MJ asked.

Dave just stood on the sideline, shaking his head. "Whose idea was this anyway?" he asked accusingly, looking at Brian.

Seeing all eyes turn toward him, Brian defended himself. "Hey, you guys know this game was supposed to be against Mr. Earl and his teacher friends. Except for Mr. Charles, I don't know where this all-star team came from. . . ."

As Brian spoke, he kept his eye on Mr. O'Shea, who was shooting free throws. He'd made seven in a row. Now eight . . . nine . . . ten.

After the last basket, Mr. O'Shea turned and strolled over to where the Bulls were grouped. "I never stop till I make ten in a row," he said. "Heh, heh."

Out of the corner of his eye, Brian caught Dave mouthing something to him. *"Don't make me vomit,"* he seemed to be saying.

Mr. O'Shea continued, "You gentlemen—" then, seeing Jo, he added with a forced smile, "—and *ladies*, want to warm up a little? Tip-off is in fifteen minutes."

"Uh, Mr. O'Shea," Brian blurted, "who are all these guys on your team? Mr. Charles is the only one I recognize."

Mr. O'Shea looked puzzled, but Brian could tell the expression was phony. "Oh, you mean, like him?" the gym teacher finally answered, nodding in the direction of the short ball-handling wizard. "That's Mr. Tamborelli. He helps develop the curriculum for all the Branford schools."

Then he pointed at the tall jump shooter. "And that's Mr. Hawkins, who runs the audiovisual services—"

"But we challenged the BFMS faculty!" Brian sputtered.

"Well, Mr. Charles teaches math, of course. And all these players are on the BFMS faculty . . . technically speaking," Mr. O'Shea replied, with a slick smile. "Maybe you just haven't met them yet. I'll be sure to introduce you."

Brian didn't know what to say next, and he looked around at the Bulls for support. MJ spoke up.

"Why aren't Ms. Darling and Dr. Byrum and the others out there shooting? Why are they just sitting on the bench?"

"You know," Mr. O'Shea answered, shaking his head, "frankly, I think they're a little *embarrassed*. They're really not quite as good as some of these other players we have on the team. But they'll see some playing time, I can assure you."

Just then a tall, muscular kid with a buzz cut came up alongside Mr. O'Shea. Brian guessed he was about fifteen years old.

"Almost ready to get started, Coach?" the boy asked.

Coach? Brian and Dave exchanged questioning glances.

"Just a few minutes, Alex," Mr. O'Shea answered. Then, to Brian and the rest of the Bulls, he said, "I'd like you to meet Alex Cox, one of my star players for Danville Prep. He'll be reffing tonight's game."

Again, Brian and Dave looked at each other, shaking their heads. The picture was getting worse and worse.

Mr. O'Shea began walking back toward the faculty basket, where the shoot-around was still in progress. Then he turned, came back to where Brian was standing, and guided him over to the corner of the gym. "Mr. Simmons, one more thing," he said, almost in a whisper.

Brian braced himself. *What else can Mr. O'Shea want?*

"Since I'm in charge of this game now," the teacher continued, "I want you to know I thought your suggestion to Mr. Earl was a good one, and we're going to use it. If the Bulls win, you'll all get A's in gym for the quarter."

Brian waited for Mr. O'Shea to finish what hc had to say.

"Of course, if you lose," the gym teacher added, with an ominous grin, "you all get F's."

CHAPTER 6

"Okay, here's what we're going to do," Jim began as the Bulls huddled around their two coaches just before the opening tip. "We're going to . . ."

A dark look of annoyance crossed his face. "Mark," Jim continued, "could you look at *me*, please?"

Jim had caught Mark staring in the direction of the other basket, where the teachers were completing their warm-up. Brian knew one of the things Jim hated most was when one of his players watched the other team instead of listening to him.

"Sorry," Mark mumbled. "It's just that they're so *tall*."

"And so *good*," Chunky added.

"Man, nothing like psyching your-selves out before we even take the floor!" Jim shouted. "Now come on! They may be big, and they may be good, but they're just a bunch of guys that have been thrown together—and I'll bet you anything they don't even let Mr. Charles touch the ball, so there are really only four players on the floor. And they've never played before as a team. That's where you have the advantage."

Brian considered what Jim was say-ing. He knew there was a little bit of truth to it. But before he could finish his thought, he heard Dave's angry voice.

"Ringers—every one of them, ex-cept for Mr. Charles. They're not even really teachers here," he complained bitterly. "It's not fair at all!"

"Hey, Droopy, life isn't always fair," Nate broke in, exasperated. "Yeah, maybe the teachers have stacked the deck a little, but now we've got to play out the hand. We've just got to out-fight them, outhustle them."

Brian could tell that behind all that rah-rah talk, both coaches also thought that the teachers had pulled a pretty cheesy move. And when he heard Jim's final pregame message— "Just try to have some fun"—he knew they might as well give up. Jim *never* talked about "just having fun" unless the game was hopeless.

As the Bulls broke their huddle and the starters headed for center court, Jo called back to the bench, "Who should we take on D?"

Jim looked at Nate for a moment, then answered, "Whoever takes *you*."

This too was out of character. Usually Jim had very specific ideas about which player each of the Bulls should guard when they played man-to-man. Obviously, in this game he realized it wouldn't make any difference.

Brian was not the least bit surprised when Mr. O'Shea sidled up alongside him and reached out to shake his hand. *I would have bet money he'd be guarding me,* Brian thought.

The six-foot-four Mr. Hawkins won the opening tip against Will without even having to leave his feet, and the ball wound up in the hands of Mr. Tamborelli. The lightning-  quick ball handler shook free from Jo, who was defending him, with an amazing crossover dribble. Fortunately for the Bulls, though, he didn't seem interested in scoring himself. Instead, he snapped a sharp bounce pass to Mr. O'Shea, who was positioned to the left of the foul line.

Brian kept one hand on Mr. O'Shea's waistband as the teacher backed him in, but it was no use. The well-built gym teacher had about a hundred pounds on him, and it was pretty hard not to give ground.

When Mr. O'Shea had bulled his

way to within eight feet of the hoop, he whirled to his left and drove around Brian for a short jump hook. The shot fell short, but Brian had grazed Mr. O'Shea's arm ever so slightly in his block attempt.

Alex Cox came flying in Brian's direction as if he were shot out of a cannon, his right arm in the air. "Foul, number sixty-seven!" the teenage referee bawled. "Two shots."

So that's *how it's going to be,* Brian thought. *If he's going to call little touch fouls like that, we might as well not even bother playing defense!*

Mr. O'Shea stepped to the line and went through what seemed to Brian to be an overdone, attention-grabbing ritual, involving adjusting his jersey, dribbling about a dozen times, taking several deep breaths, and sighting the front rim with his left hand.

The gym teacher *did* drain both free throws, though.

Mr. O'Shea grinned broadly at Brian as he jogged backward to his defensive end of the floor. "Just a suggestion, Mr. Simmons," Mr. O'Shea offered in a buddy-buddy voice. "You don't want to send me to the line too often." He winked at Brian. "I never miss."

Is this guy sickening, or what? Brian thought.

Dave brought the ball up slowly, deliberately. His usual flair was missing. He faked to Jo on the wing, then worked a bounce pass into Will in the pivot. Will wheeled and went up for his dependable fall-away jumper.

Mr. Hawkins rejected Will's shot with a resounding slap. Brian noticed that, again, Mr. Hawkins hadn't even had to jump.

Will looked stunned. He wasn't used to playing against anyone taller than he was, and he *certainly* wasn't used to getting his shot blocked.

"Oh, *that's* cool," Brian heard Will's brother say angrily to Nate on the sideline. "A six-foot-four teacher thinks he's a big man because he can send back a fifth-grader's shot!"

"Maybe we ought to put *ourselves* into the game," Nate replied, equally furious. "Even things up a little."

Brian noticed that Mr. Hawkins was looking a little sheepish after the block—and after the fuss the coaches made over it. Mr. Charles shook his head and sighed as he jogged up the sideline.

The teachers' thin, red-haired shooting guard picked up the loose ball and handed it off to Mr. Tamborelli. The point guard dribbled across mid-court to the top of the key, then held the ball over his head with two hands. Jo dropped off him just a little bit, watching for the pass. But Mr. Tamborelli, seeing his defender was giving him a little breathing room, calmly banged in the eighteen-footer.

The teachers led 4–0.

Down by four less than a minute into the game, Brian began to panic, but he heard Nate calmly call out, "All right, Bulls, settle down. Set up your offense."

The Bulls worked the ball around as patiently as they could. Finally, Derek set a screen for Brian in the left corner, his favorite spot. But as Brian was about to pull the trigger, he saw Mr. O'Shea come flying at him, and he rushed his release slightly. His shot bounced off the front of the rim.

Mr. Charles managed to awkwardly grab the rebound. He quickly tossed it to Mr. Tamborelli. The point guard pushed the ball upcourt and quickly hit Mr. Hawkins with a bullet pass in the left corner. Mr. Hawkins squared up to shoot, checked his feet, took a step back beyond the circle, and fired.

Alex Cox, the referee, made a big show of throwing his arms up in the air. "Three!" he shouted.

With the score now 7–0, Jim immediately asked for a time-out. As both teams headed to the sidelines, Brian saw Nate corner Mr. O'Shea on his way to the teachers' bench.

"You planning on giving Ms. Darling and Mr. Dupont any playing time, or are they just along for the ride?" Brian heard Nate challenge sarcastically.

"Calm down, Bowman," Mr. O'Shea answered, with a smile on his face but a hard edge in his voice. "They'll play. It's still early in the first quarter. Our starters haven't even broken a sweat yet." With a nasty twinkle in his eye, he added, "There's still *lots* of time left. And before this game is over, at least *one* of your players is going to learn a little lesson about respect."

Brian felt a chill. Though Mr. O'Shea had been talking to Nate, the teacher was staring straight at *him*.

In the Bulls' huddle, Jim told the team that the teachers were bound to cool off, and that they, the Bulls, had gotten off to slow starts before. But Brian knew that there was really nothing helpful that Jim or Nate could say.

The Bulls were simply overmatched.

Within seconds after the time-out, Derek, a determined look on his face, drove the lane for a layup—the Bulls' first score of the game.

Brian felt a sense of relief as he dropped back on defense. He looked at Mr. O'Shea's face, expecting to see at least a half smile, maybe a look that would say, *Hey, you guys finally scored!*

Instead, he saw Mr. O'Shea's jaw set, his eyes narrow, his whole face harden. Brian couldn't believe it: Mr. O'Shea was offended that the Bulls had even scored one hoop! *What was this maniac expecting—that his team of hotshots was going to shut us out?* Brian wondered in amazement.

Mr. O'Shea inbounded to Mr. Tamborelli, then took the return pass just past the mid-court line. He dribbled right at Brian. Brian got up on the balls of his feet, ready for the gym teacher to drive to the left or the right. But instead of trying to blow by him, Mr. O'Shea stopped and popped from just above the foul line.

It had taken the teachers all of five seconds to get back the basket Derek had scored. The score was 9–2, and Brian sensed that Mr. O'Shea, if anything, was playing *harder* now than he was at the start.

Jo brought the ball up with a sense of urgency for the Bulls, but before she could make an entry pass to Will, she was stripped by the flashing hands of Mr. Tamborelli. And though the point guard had seemed content to dish earlier, now he didn't hesitate to go coast-to-coast for the uncontested layup.

"Come on, you big bullies!" an angry parent called out from the stands. "What are you guys trying to prove?"

The teachers led 11–2.

As Dave dribbled the ball into the frontcourt for the Bulls, Brian heard Jim call out for the team to slow it down. The coach was signaling for a set play.

Three quick passes resulted in what looked like an open eight-footer in the lane for Will, but at the last moment Mr. Hawkins extended his long arms, and Will had to change his shot.

No good.

Mr. Hawkins picked off the easy rebound and threw the outlet to Mr.

Tamborelli, who delivered a long pass upcourt to the power forward. Derek had alertly gotten back on defense, but the bulky teacher used his height and weight advantage against the Bulls' best player, muscling his way in for an easy four-foot bank shot.

The contact on the play knocked Derek to the floor. As the teacher pulled Derek back up, Brian heard him mumble, "Sorry." Brian also thought he looked a little uncomfortable—the way Mr. Hawkins had looked after blocking Will's shot. *Maybe Mr. O'Shea is the only one who's really enjoying this mismatch,* it occurred to Brian.

With the first quarter winding down, the Bulls were behind 13–2.

The deafening noise level in the gym had dropped off to near silence. Kristen Albert and her friends were no longer stomping and cheering. They sat with stunned looks on their faces.

Parents were muttering to one another, looking none too happy. Brian saw his own mother and father talking to each other with concerned expressions, but he couldn't make out what they were saying.

Brian glanced over at the Bulls' bench. Mark, Chunky, and MJ sat slumped over, staring at the floor. Jim shook his head slowly back and forth, arms folded in front of his chest. Nate paced the sideline, up and back, up and back, a murderous look on his face.

This isn't exactly the game we were all expecting, Brian reflected miserably.

CHAPTER 7

The coaches took a different, more realistic approach during the brief pause between quarters. They no longer tried to make the Bulls believe that effort and unity could earn them a win against this taller, stronger team. Jim said flat-out that Mr. O'Shea had cheated in pulling together this group of ringers, and that there was no way a group of eleven-year-olds was going to beat them.

"But we came to play," an angered Nate added as he continued to pace the sideline, "so let's *play*. Even if we can't beat 'em, let's at least show 'em what Bulls basketball is all about."

Though Brian was still upset about how the game he and Mr. Earl cooked up had turned out, the straight talk from Jim and Nate picked him up a bit. He walked out on the floor for the second quarter ready to do some damage.

The Bulls had first possession in the new period, and Jo inbounded to Dave to start the action. Dave advanced to the top of the key, then held the ball over his head before firing a two-hand pass to Brian on his left.

Mr. O'Shea was guarding Brian closely—almost chest-to-chest. Though the teachers led 13–2, Brian could still see that look of grim determination in Mr. O'Shea's eyes, and knew he had no intention of letting up.

Brian pump faked. As he'd figured, Mr. O'Shea was so eager to block his shot that he fell for the fake, leaping at Brian—and right by him. Momentarily free from his defender, Brian hit the open jumper.

But he soon realized that making Mr. O'Shea look bad had been a dangerous move. On the teachers' very next possession, Mr. O'Shea drove in Brian's direction and barreled him right over. Brian crumpled to the floor, and Mr. O'Shea continued on to score the layup.

As Brian lay in pain on the hard wood surface, holding his thigh where he'd been kneed by Mr. O'Shea, he was amazed to see Alex Cox come flying at him. "The basket's good—and a blocking foul on number sixty-seven!" the referee shouted.

What? This sleazeball doesn't call the charge on Mr. O'Shea, Brian thought in disbelief, *and then he has the nerve to count the basket and call a foul on me?*

The bleachers erupted with the sound of parents and kids booing. Dr. Byrum jumped to his feet, a pained look on his face. Mr. Charles hung his head, his pale legs glaring under the gym lights.

Nate came sprinting out onto the floor to make sure Brian was all right and to give the referee a piece of his mind. But as soon as the tall coach opened his mouth, Alex chopped his two hands together in a T—indicating a technical foul on Nate!

Brian was afraid Nate was going to haul off and punch the fifteen-year-old, but fortunately Jim ran out and stepped between them. He was able to say something to Nate to calm him down, and then steered him back to the bench.

Despite the furor, Mr. O'Shea calmly made both free throws—the technical, and the one for Brian's "foul."

The teachers led 17–4.

After the incident between Mr. O'Shea and Brian, the game got even more out of hand. The pushing and shoving became constant, and none of it was called—at least none of it was called against the teachers.

The restlessness and unruliness spread to the stands as well. Parents who had been whispering in pairs were now banded together in clusters, openly hooting the referee's calls and the physical play of the faculty. Brian saw the angry look on both his parents' faces and hoped his father wouldn't do anything to embarrass him.

Midway through the second quarter, Dave, who was guarding Mr. Tamborelli, was crunched by an illegal pick set by Mr. Hawkins. But there was no whistle, and Mr. Tamborelli scored, upping the teachers' lead to 22–6. Brian saw Mr. Hawkins apologize to Dave, but so what? The basket still counted!

Brian was infuriated by the no-call.

"What about that moving pick?" he screamed at Alex Cox.

Cox walked right up to Brian, face-to-face, and gave him an innocent smile. "Sorry," he said. "Didn't see it."

As the Bulls jogged upcourt to their offensive end, Brian glanced over at Ms. Darling, Mr. Dupont, Dr. Byrum, and the other "real" teachers. None of them had gotten into the game yet. He caught Dr. Byrum's eye.

"Can't you do anything about this?" he pleaded, slowing down as he ran by.

The always-smiling principal looked absolutely grim.

"I gave Mr. O'Shea *and* the ref a little talking-to between quarters," he answered. "I warned them to watch it—that things were getting out of hand. But I agreed to let Mr. O'Shea run the show, and he *does* have Mr. Charles out there playing for the teachers. Besides, this is a fund-raiser. I can't really call the whole thing off in the middle. I'm not happy about this, though. I can assure you of that."

Brian couldn't believe that Mr. O'Shea seemed to have no fear of the principal. *Dr. Byrum could have him fired*, Brian thought. *Man, this guy must really want to beat us bad!*

With less than two minutes remaining in the half and the Bulls down 29–10, Derek drove boldly to the hoop but was fouled hard by Mr. O'Shea and sent sprawling out of bounds.

Brian rushed over to help up his teammate, but a short, well-muscled man in a navy warm-up suit had beaten him to it. Brian would have recognized that barrel chest and narrow waist anywhere.

It was Mr. Earl.

Mr. O'Shea spotted the older gym teacher at the same time Brian did.

His face, red from exertion, turned pale.

"What are you doing here?" Mr. O'Shea sputtered. Brian had never seen him look so rattled.

Mr. Earl fixed him with a cold, hard gaze.

"It was my turn to speak before dinner," Mr. Earl said, "and I cut out as soon as my speech was finished. I always knew I had a shot at making it back here for the second half, but I didn't want to tell the kids that and risk disappointing them."

As he spoke, Mr. Earl looked around the gym—taking in the lopsided count on the scoreboard, the strange cast of characters assembled on the floor for the "teachers" team, the downcast expressions on the Bulls' faces. Brian was pretty sure Mr. Earl got the picture.

The older gym teacher pulled Mr. O'Shea off into a corner. Though Mr. Earl was trying his best to keep the conversation private, anger made his voice rise, and Brian was able to catch most of what was being said.

"Now I have a question for *you*," Brian heard Mr. Earl demand in an accusing tone. "What *exactly* is going on here?"

"What do you mean?" Mr. O'Shea replied. Brian could tell he was stalling for time to think.

"You know what I mean," Mr. Earl pressed on. "I see Mr. Charles, standing over there with that embarrassed expression on his face. But who are these *other* players, for one thing?"

"Well," Mr. O'Shea began slowly, "there's Mr. Tamborelli here, who's on the curriculum committee—"

"I *know* who they *are!*" Mr. Earl hissed. "What I want to know is, what are they *doing* here?"

Mr. O'Shea looked all around the gym, as if he might find an excuse on the tumbling mats behind the baskets or the banners hanging from the rafters.

Mr. Earl shook his head and gave the younger gym teacher a reproving look. "This was supposed to be a Bulls versus BFMS faculty game—for fun," he said. "We didn't need you to bring in a bunch of ringers. Was showing up these fifth-graders really that important to you?"

Mr. O'Shea didn't answer. He hung his head for a moment, and then stalked off to the sideline.

Mr. Earl walked back to the center of the floor. He motioned to the sweaty "teachers" on the floor, who had not only started but played the whole game so far. "Why don't you guys take a rest?" Mr. Earl suggested in a no-nonsense tone. "Mr. Charles, you can stay in if you want."

Mr. Charles gave Mr. Earl an enthusiastic thumbs-up sign.

Then Mr. Earl went over to the teachers' bench, where Ms. Darling, Mr. Dupont, and Dr. Byrum were sitting.

"You three, get ready to check in," Mr. Earl ordered. "From this point on, we'll play with just the teachers who actually *teach* here."

"All right!" Brian heard several of the Bulls shout.

As Mr. Earl shed his warm-up suit, he saw Mr. O'Shea heading back out onto the floor. "You can have a seat too," he said to the other gym teacher. "I'll be the fifth for a while."

Alex Cox looked at his coach with a questioning expression, as if to say, *With you out, am I still supposed to be reffing this game?*

Mr. Earl answered the unspoken question for him. "You, son," he said, "I've already seen enough of your calls. You're dismissed."

He took the whistle from Alex Cox and walked over to where Nate was standing. "Bowman," he said, in a low, confidential voice, "your dad in the building by any chance?"

Nate winked at the gym teacher. "You kidding? Of *course* he's in the building. You think my dad would miss this game?"

Nate located his father in the bleachers and motioned for him to come down. The pudgy, balding shop-keeper, a big-time ballplayer in his day, made his way carefully down the bleacher steps. He still lived and breathed basketball—though now mostly through his son and through the Branford Bulls.

As Nate Bowman, Sr. reached the gym floor, Mr. Earl held out the whistle to him. "Mind taking over the reffing chores, Mr. Bowman? Word has it you know a thing or two about hoops."

A broad smile spread across the elder Bowman's face. "My pleasure," he beamed, flattered to be asked.

Brian noticed that Mr. Bowman wasn't the only one smiling. For the first time since the opening tip, Brian saw big grins on the faces of Ms. Darling, Mr. Dupont, Dr. Byrum, and Mr. Charles. All the Bulls looked psyched and ready to play. The parents in the bleachers looked happy too, as did all the other students in the stands. And Kristen Albert and her friends were waving their poster and chanting, "Let's go Bulls!" again.

Now this, Brian thought, *is more like it!*

"As my first official act as referee," Mr. Bowman said, "I'm going to declare that this is the beginning of the second half—because we've had quite enough of the shenanigans that went on in the first half! And I'm also going to wipe out the score—"

"No, Mr. Bowman!" Dave objected. "Leave the score at 29–10. We can catch these sorry dudes. It'll be more of a challenge this way."

"Yeah!" all the Bulls agreed.

"Okay, Droopy, have it your way," Mr. Bowman said, using Dave's nickname, "but I *am* going to award my man Derek three free throws—"

"*Three?*" Mr. Earl asked, pretending to be outraged.

"That's right, three," Mr. Bowman replied to his friend, in a mock-scolding voice. "That was one nasty foul Mr. O'Shea laid on him."

Derek stepped to the line, adjusted his wristbands, and without saying a word, drained his three free throws.

"Twenty-nine, thirteen!" Dave announced. "Look at that, Mr. Earl. No time off the clock, and your lead's already going up in smoke."

"Hold on to your shorts, Danzig, you haven't seen Earl the Pearl in action yet," Mr. Earl responded.

Mr. Earl received the inbounds pass and dribbled the ball upcourt for the teachers with a steady grace. Brian had to admit, he definitely looked like he knew what he was doing.

But when he passed the ball to Dr. Byrum, it was a different story. The potbellied principal bounced the ball once, then gathered it in against his flabby midsection. Brian could tell he wasn't at all comfortable handling the ball. At his first opportunity, Dr. Byrum shuffled off a pass to Mr. Charles.

"Shoot!" Ms. Darling screeched, and without hesitation, Mr. Charles obeyed.

Brian had never seen anything quite like it in his life.

Mr. Charles heaved the ball underhanded, with two hands. His shot landed about ten feet to the left of the basket.

"Whoa—I haven't seen that shooting style since Rick Barry—but he used to make 'em," Nate laughed, a wide grin on his face.

Will picked up on the good-natured ribbing. "Calling that shot an airball would be a *compliment*, Mr. Charles. I think maybe you ought to stick to algebra."

Mr. Charles smiled. "Watch it!" he called back. "I can get my *earlier* teammates back out here, you know!"

"Anything but that!" Will yelled.

Meanwhile, Brian had retrieved the off-target shot and was dribbling nonchalantly upcourt.

"Come on, Brian, try to get by me," Ms. Darling challenged. She was crouched down in what she seemed to think was a proper defensive position.

Brian had to laugh. Though in the classroom she was one of the prettiest teachers in the school, on the basketball court Ms. Darling looked comical. Her white BFMS T-shirt was so huge, it all but covered her knee-length leggings. She bounced around on the balls of her feet, trying to appear menacing, but Brian thought she looked more like a jumping bean than a tough defender.

"Come on, hot stuff," she egged him on again.

With a lazy, high dribble, Brian lured her into attempting a steal. Then he whipped around and blew by the off-balance teacher for an easy layup.

"Now you see me, now you don't," he boasted.

"Way to school her, Bri-Bri!"

Brian looked up into the bleachers and saw the twins jumping up and down. He wasn't sure if it was Todd or Allie who had called out—or both.

His smooth move had brought Kristen and her friends to their feet too. "Simmons, Simmons, he's our man . . . ," they chanted, with Kristen leading the cheer. Brian felt his face flush.

He also noticed that all the parents looked relaxed again. Everyone was having a good time. *Guess this game was a pretty decent idea after all,* Brian thought proudly.

Mr. Earl advanced the ball past mid-court for the teachers, then sent a bounce pass to Mr. Dupont, the social studies teacher. Brian could see by Mr. Earl's passing pattern that he was trying to get all the teachers involved in the game.

Mr. Dupont had on the same ridiculous shiny blue satin shorts he'd worn to practice earlier in the week, and his white socks were again hiked up to his knees. Brian couldn't decide who looked nerdier—Mr. Charles or Mr. Dupont.

Like most of the teachers, Mr. Dupont seemed to be afraid to dribble. From right where he stood—well beyond the three-point circle—he let loose one of his old-fashioned, from-the-belly-button two-hand set shots.

Brian followed the high arc of the shot with amazement . . .

Jo broke out singing, "Happy birthday to you . . ." and all the Bulls joined in. Mr. Dupont had a puzzled look on his face.

"What, it's not your birthday today?" Dave asked the social studies teacher.

"No, my birthday's not until—oh, I get it," Mr. Dupont said, hitting himself on the head. "That shot was my *birthday present*. Very funny."

The Bulls answered his freak shot back immediately with another score. This time it was Chunky, who hit on a short turnaround jumper, a shot he'd learned from Will.

As Mr. Earl began dribbling up-court again for the teachers, Dave said, "Hey, how 'bout letting someone else bring up the ball?"

"Yeah," Brian chimed in, "we want to see Ms. Darling dribble."

"No, Mr. Earl," the English teacher objected, "you keep it. I don't want to make these boys look bad."

But in spite of her reluctance, Mr.

Earl gave the ball up to Ms. Darling. She began desperately slapping at it with two hands, just the way she had at practice.

Brian, Dave, and MJ all fell to the floor in hysterics. Will walked over to Mr. Bowman. "Excuse me, but isn't that double dribble?" he asked.

"No, Too-Tall, you've got it all wrong," Mr. Bowman said, trying to keep a straight face. He *always* addressed the Bulls by the nicknames he'd given them. "If Ms. Darling can dribble with two hands, that just means she's twice as good."

In the midst of all the laughter from the Bulls and the teachers alike, Brian noticed Mr. O'Shea at the far corner of the gym, packing up his duffel bag. Without saying a word to anyone, the young gym teacher stormed out of the building.

Brian saw that Mr. Earl had been watching too.

"He looked pretty upset," Brian observed.

Mr. Earl nodded his head slowly. "Not as upset as he's going to be when I talk to him in my office Monday morning."

Bowman's Market was packed.

Not only were all the Bulls there—as usual, after a game—but all their parents, a few other friends, and the "real" BFMS teachers, as well.

Mr. Bowman scurried around, busily hauling out extra chairs to help more people fit around the booths, a proud smile on his face.

"So I guess we all get A's in gym, isn't that right, Mr. Earl?" Brian teased from his counter stool. He had a happy grin plastered on his face from being congratulated so many times by other BFMS students.

"No, you know I never went along with that," Mr. Earl answered, "but you certainly have earned your free sodas. Okay, Mr. Bowman?"

Brian smiled, but then a troubled look crossed his face. The gym teacher noticed his changed expression. "Something bothering you, Brian?" Mr. Earl asked.

"Not really," Brian answered. "It's just that after you kicked Mr. O'Shea out . . . I felt like you kind of *handed* us the game."

"Not at all!" Mr. Earl protested. "That team of semipros Mr. O'Shea put together—that's not the team you had challenged, and that's not the kind of game you bargained for."

"You can say *that* again," Brian agreed.

"The second half," Mr. Earl continued, "when Mr. Dupont and Ms. Darling and Dr. Byrum and I took over—that's what the Bulls–faculty game was supposed to be all about. Old-fashioned fun, for a good cause. And I gotta hand it to you, Brian, you Bulls beat us fair and square."

"Oh, I don't know how fair it was when Dave stole the ball every time I managed to get my hands on it," Ms. Darling put in, trying to sound huffy.

"And when Brian blocked my old reliable two-hand set shot," Mr. Dupont added.

Dave had been listening intently to the conversation between Brian and the teachers.

"You know, Mr. Earl," he began, grinning slyly. "We may dis you a lot, but after seeing you play, I have to admit, your hang time really isn't bad at all."

Mr. Earl perked up at the compliment. "Really?" he asked, flattered.

"Well, let's put it this way," Brian concluded, picking up on Dave's cue. "If I got down on my belly, with my face on the ground, I actually might see just a little bit of daylight between the floor and your sneakers when you take off."

Mr. Earl's face fell. He looked down at his shoes.

"You know," he said in a subdued voice, "sometimes you boys ought to think of other people's feelings a little before making jokes at their expense."

Brian felt a jolt in the pit of his stomach. "But Mr. Earl," he replied, "we were only—"

With a twinkle in his eye and a huge grin on his face, Mr. Earl pointed at Dave and Brian.

"Gotcha!" he said.

Don't miss Book #1 in the Super Hoops college championship miniseries: #10, **Foul!** Coming soon!

Dave, sensing the opportunity for a fast break, went streaking toward the Bulls' basket. The always-alert Derek hit him with a one-hand outlet pass. With no white Wildcats' jersey between him and the basket, Dave figured he was home free.

But just before he reached the hoop, he looked over his shoulder and saw Jason Fox bearing down on him. Jason had no chance to block the shot, but as Dave left the ground for the layup, Jason hammered him from behind. Dave was sent sprawling to the hard wood floor.

Before the referee could even get his arm in the air and call the obvious two-shot foul on Fox, Dave had picked himself off the floor and charged the Wildcats' forward.

"What do you think you're doing?" Dave exploded, as he shoved Fox hard in the chest with two hands, sending him reeling backward toward the bleachers.

About the Author

Hank Herman is a writer and newspaper columnist who lives in Connecticut with his wife, Carol, and their three sons, Matt, Greg, and Robby.

His column, "The Home Team," appears in the *Westport News*. It's about kids, sports, and life in the suburbs.

Although Mr. Herman was formerly the editor in chief of *Health* magazine, he now writes mostly about sports. At one time, he was a tennis teacher, and he has also run the New York City Marathon. He coaches kids' basketball every winter and Little League baseball every spring.

He runs, bicycles, skis, kayaks, and plays tennis and basketball on a regular basis. Mr. Herman admits that he probably spends about as much time playing, coaching, and following sports as he does writing.

Of all sports, basketball is his favorite.